Her Father's ❈ Garden ❈

James Vollbracht
Illustrated by Janet Brooke

WISDOM
Children's Books

Wisdom Publications · Boston

To Kuan Yin

The publisher gratefully acknowledges the generous help of the Hershey Family Foundation in sponsoring the production of this book.

Wisdom Publications
361 Newbury Street
Boston, Massachusetts 02115
USA

Library of Congress Cataloging-in-Publication Data

Vollbracht, James R., 1950–
      Her father's garden / James Vollbracht ; illustrated by Janet Brooke.
            p.   cm.
      Summary: Mi Shan, the gentle daughter of the Innkeeper in the Village
High Above the White Clouds, transforms those she meets by enabling them to see their better natures and comparing them to plants in the garden of her father's dreams.
      ISBN 0-86171-117-3
      [1. Conduct of life—Fiction.   2. Caring—Fiction.   3. Gardens—
Fiction.]   I. Brooke, Janet, ill.   II. Title.
PZ7.V8865He   1996
[Fic]—dc20   96–21706
                                                                                                          AC

ISBN 0 86171 117 3

01 00 99 98 97
  6   5   4   3   2

Designed by: L·J·Sawlit *&* Adie Russell

Printed in the United States of America.

Long ago,

far beyond the clatter of the Great Cities, on a mountain pass where the winds of the world swirl over the highest peaks, in the Village High Above the White Clouds lived Mi Shan, daughter of the innkeeper.

It was said by the townspeople that on the morning Mi Shan was born, a pure white songbird sang a song so wondrous that everyone who heard it stopped what they were doing, as if in a dream, to listen.

"It was a song so beautiful," they said, "that for a moment Heaven and Earth seemed as one."

3

As a small girl, Mi Shan loved to help her father with the chores at the inn. At the end of each day, she happily scrubbed the large, wooden tables and polished the big, black rice kettles until they shone. Although she seldom spoke to anyone but her father, her kind and gentle ways were well known to all.

Each morning, very early, Mi Shan began her chores. Scooping up the leaky wooden buckets, she hurried to fetch water at the town well. As she passed the broken-down shops, the high mountain winds whistled a haunting tune through the torn rice-paper windows. The splintered sign of the village official, who had left in disgust years before, lay on the frozen ground. The untended, tattered prayer flags, reminders that monks from the great monastery had once journeyed this way, flapped noisily in the wind.

When Mi Shan saw the townspeople, she smiled and nodded cheerfully, but they could only grumble and complain, "What is there to smile about? We live in a village that is so high nothing ever grows." Some even muttered, "It is so cold here that even the yaks' milk freezes if it isn't stored in the sun!" Others nodded and said, "Yes, it is a place where no one belongs."

When the days grew longer and the snows blocking the high mountain passes began to melt, the first caravans from the Great Cities arrived. The Village suddenly sprang to life. The townspeople crowded into the inn to hear news from the Great Cities, and Mi Shan brought them all huge bowls brimming with fragrant white rice and endless cups of wild ginseng tea. She greeted those from the caravans with a smile and a nod, but her shyness caused them to shrug and say, "Who is this girl? She never says a word!"

The townspeople just shook their heads and replied, "Oh, pay no attention to her. It is only Mi Shan. She was born on a morning when a pure white songbird sang an unforgettable song, yet she hardly ever speaks and seems to live in a world of her own. We call her the quiet one."

After everyone went home and the tables were washed and the rice kettles polished, Mi Shan climbed the creaky stairs to her father's room. There, she and her father sat before the fire and shared cups of hot jasmine tea, and talked long into the night.

At times, they would just sit together in silence. During these moments, Mi Shan's and her father's most heartfelt dreams would come to life and fill the room.

One evening, Mi Shan's father gazed out the window at a crescent moon resting on the mountain peaks. With a faraway look in his eye he said, "Mi Shan, for the past many nights I have dreamed of a garden. A garden more beautiful than anyone has ever seen. A garden," he said softly, "of hopes and dreams." Taking her hand in his, he began to describe each bush, flower, vine, and tree in the garden. When he finished, he closed his eyes and whispered, "One day, people from the Great Cities will come to the Village High Above the White Clouds to see this garden, for it will grow in the ground behind the inn. They will make the difficult climb up the mountain, for the promise of the garden will call to them again and again."

Night after night, Mi Shan asked her father to tell the story of the garden. Each time she heard the story, the garden became more real. But something troubled Mi Shan deeply. One evening, after her father had described the garden in great

detail, Mi Shan quietly said, "Father, the garden is so alive in our hearts, but everyone in the Village says it is far too cold for anything to grow here. They say that nothing good could ever come from the Village High Above the White Clouds. They say that only fools live in this Village, and that if they had their wits about them, they would leave!"

Mi Shan's father nodded knowingly, his face still bright with the beauty of the dream. "I know what people say and what appears to be. But always keep your highest hope and highest dream alive within your heart. Remember, Mi Shan, things are not always what they seem!"

The very next morning the townspeople in the Village High Above the White Clouds shook their heads and rubbed their eyes. For there, behind the inn, was Mi Shan on her knees, digging tiny holes in the frozen ground and planting seeds! As a light spring snow began to fall, some of the village boys laughed and pointed at Mi Shan and called her names. The villagers shook their heads disapprovingly and said, "Ah, poor Mi Shan! It must be the high mountain air that makes her like this. She truly lives in a world of her own."

One afternoon, soon after, when the inn was very full, a loud argument broke out between two of the caravan leaders. One of the men was much smaller than the other. Fearing for the smaller man, Mi Shan rushed over to the old soldier who sat at the same table with his friends every day. "Great Warrior," she said quietly, "I hear that you have fought in many battles and are very strong. Won't you help bring this argument to an end?"

The old soldier and his friends looked at one another in astonishment! No one had ever heard Mi Shan speak like this before! All waited eagerly for the old soldier's reply. Finally, the old soldier grunted and said, "Why should I stop this argument? This is no business of mine!"

After hesitating a moment, Mi Shan replied, "Because you, Great Warrior, are like the mighty tree in my father's garden. Your arms are like powerful boughs that protect those who are not as strong."

His friends howled! "You, a mighty tree?" they shouted, "The last battle you fought was ages ago! You have no heart to fight again!"

Yet while they laughed, the old soldier's eyes

stayed fixed on Mi Shan. "It may be true that you have not fought in a battle for some time," she told him, "but mighty trees never lose their strength of heart, and they always protect those who are in need!" Mi Shan's words stirred something deep inside the old soldier. Ignoring his friends' laughter, he rose from the table and, by his stern and powerful presence, quickly brought the argument to an end.

The whole inn was quiet as the old soldier trudged back to his seat. As he passed the last table, the rich merchant laughed loudly. Turning to Mi Shan, he bellowed, "And what am I like, Mi Shan? If *he* is a mighty tree, then *I* must be the sun!"

Nobody moved or dared even to breathe. This was the most powerful man in the Village. To offend him would be very dangerous! Mi Shan gazed at the merchant for just a moment, and then, looking down, said, "Rich merchant, you are not like the sun at all!"

"What?" shouted the merchant. "What do you mean?"

Mi Shan continued gazing at the floor as she shyly replied, "Because you have so much wealth, you are more like the cool, clear stream in my father's garden. Your waters bring life to all the plants in need. Because you give and share what you have, you are truly great indeed!" Mi Shan then bowed and was gone.

The rich merchant sat stunned by Mi Shan's words. Those in the inn dared not laugh as they had with the old soldier, and turned back to their rice and tea. Then, the rich merchant stood up and shouted, "Yes, to be like a cool, clear stream, that is a very great honor!" As he stomped proudly out of the inn, everyone was amazed to see him drop a gold coin in the bowl of the old village beggar, who smiled in return.

That afternoon, the entire village was humming with the news of what had happened at the inn. "Ah, poor Mi Shan," they said, "when she finally speaks, she tells of a garden that doesn't even exist!"

Then they chuckled, "Even the old soldier and the rich merchant were enchanted by her dream for a moment or two." Yet, as the days went by, the townspeople scratched their heads as the old soldier broke up two more fights at the inn, and the rich merchant started giving away blankets to everyone in need.

One day, as Mi Shan was waiting for her turn at the village well, she noticed that the town milkmaid was standing in line with tears running down her cheeks. The milkmaid looked as though she carried the weight of a thousand stones upon her back. Moving to her side so no one else could hear, Mi Shan inquired, "My friend, why is your heart so heavy?"

At first the milkmaid shook her head and said nothing, but as tears filled her eyes, she turned to Mi Shan and whispered, "Oh, Mi Shan, I am just a milkmaid! No one ever seems to notice me. I have grown up in the mountains far away from the village, and I don't know how to act or what to say around the others. When I try to speak, I stutter and say foolish things!"

Mi Shan looked lovingly at the milkmaid. "That is because you are like the tiny lilies-of-the-valley in my father's garden. Although they are among the loveliest flowers, they often get lost in the shadows of the vines and trees and go unnoticed!" Surprised at her words, the milkmaid glanced up at Mi Shan, who continued, "Each flower in my father's garden has its own special gift to give. No one flower is greater than another. Yes, the lilies-of-the-valley are oftentimes unnoticed, but they fill the garden with the sweetest fragrance."

A shy smile began to appear on the milkmaid's face, and the heavy weight she carried started to disappear. As tears of joy trickled down the milk-maid's cheek, she squeezed Mi Shan's hand for a moment. Then, snatching up her pails, she rushed after some of the village girls who were coming down the path.

As one season passed into the next, those in the caravans started telling stories in the Great Cities about the Village High Above the White Clouds. They told of a girl who spoke only of a garden and who planted seeds in the snow! They spoke of a rich merchant who gave away blankets, and of an old soldier who stopped fights all around the village. Sheepishly they said, "Even the milk from their yaks seems to taste especially sweet!"

Those in the Great Cities threw back their heads and laughed, "Surely," they said, "the high mountain air must have gone to your heads for you to believe such things! Everyone knows that there is no such place as that!"

Yet, as time passed, Mi Shan continued to tend her father's garden every day. Some of the villagers

still chuckled when they saw her planting even more seeds, but others would secretly ask her what special plant or flower they were in the garden.

To the boys who ran through the streets creating mischief, Mi Shan called after them, "Ah, you are like the wildflowers in my father's garden. Be sure not to get mixed in with the weeds!"

To the girls who washed clothes in the clear pools in the mountain meadows and gossiped about everyone in the Village, she said, "You are like the lilacs in my father's garden, blowing in the mountain winds. The lilacs hear many secrets but keep them to themselves. In the garden, they whisper only of the beauty of the other flowers, and that makes them even more beautiful in turn."

One evening, as Mi Shan was busy sweeping the floor of the inn, she saw the woodcutter's son slumped over a table with his head in his hands. As Mi Shan approached, he raised his head and said, "Mi Shan, may I speak with you?" Mi Shan nodded and sat down next to him. Tears gathered in the boy's eyes as he said, "I can never do enough to please my father. If I chop three piles of wood, he says I should have done four. If I work until the sun goes down, he says I am lazy and should work until the moon is high. Mi Shan, whatever I do, it is never good enough. Help me, Mi Shan!"

Suddenly, the door of the inn flew open. It was the woodcutter. Quickly spotting his son, he shouted, "So, there you are!"

As the woodcutter stomped toward the table, Mi Shan bowed to him and said, "O great woodcutter, your son was just telling me all about you."

"He was?" said the woodcutter, surprised.

"Oh yes," said Mi Shan boldly. "He tells me that you are the hardest worker he knows. By coming to the inn, it also shows that you are very wise."

"It does?" said the woodcutter, a bit confused.

"Oh yes," replied Mi Shan. "By coming to the

inn you show us that there is a time to work and a time to rest. That, of course, is very wise indeed!"

Taking in her words, the woodcutter's face began to soften. Pleased with himself, he said quietly, "Why, yes, yes it is."

Mi Shan stood up quickly and offered her chair to the woodcutter. "Come, woodcutter," Mi Shan said. "Come sit by your son, and I shall bring you some hot, wild root tea."

While Mi Shan poured the tea, she said, "Yes, I shall make this table ready each evening at sunset for the woodcutter and his son. For you are like the vines in my father's garden. You know that by day you reach for the sunlight and work, while at night you gaze at the stars and dream of what could be." With that, Mi Shan bowed and returned to her sweeping.

The woodcutter began sipping his tea. After his third cup, he took a deep breath and pulled his chair close to his son. For the first time in his life, the woodcutter put his arm around his son and said, "Tell me your dreams."

Years passed, and the whole village gradually fell under the spell of the garden. Mi Shan referred to the village elders as the sturdy bushes and the high hedges that bordered the garden to keep it safe. She reverently called the priests, who rang the temple bells each morning, the forget-me-nots, because they reminded everyone of their true home. She called the newborn children baby's breath, and their mothers, the deep blue meadow grasses from which they grew. Now, when the villagers saw Mi Shan digging in the snow-covered ground behind the inn, they would kindly say, "Dear Mi Shan, she means well. Let us hope that one day her garden will bloom!"

Early one morning, just before the sun appeared over the mountains, Mi Shan, who had worked all night scrubbing the floors of the inn, stood gazing hopelessly at the barren ground behind the inn. More exhausted than usual from her work, she began to wonder for the first time, "Perhaps I am foolish to believe in this garden. After all, it is only a garden of dreams!"

Sinking to her knees, she searched the frozen earth for some sign of life. Finding none, she slowly sank to the frozen ground and fell into a deep and weary sleep. The old soldier, who had risen early that morning, saw her lying on the ground and came rushing to her side. Cradling her in his strong arms, he first gently called her name and then, with his booming voice, shouted for all the Village to hear, "Our Mi Shan is ill! Our Mi Shan is ill! Everyone come!"

The whole village heard his call and came running! The rich merchant appeared with a cup of cool water. Then came the milkmaid, the laundry girls, the temple priests, the mothers with their children, the woodcutter and his son, and everyone whose life had been touched by Mi Shan. As the rich merchant held the cup of water to Mi Shan's lips, all of the villagers closed their eyes to say a heartfelt prayer of love and hope for their dear friend.

Just then, the great winds that rush across the mountains became very calm. In that moment just before dawn, when all things are possible, everyone in the garden heard the first notes of a song.

It was the same song that many of them had heard on the morning that Mi Shan was born! A song so beautiful that, as they listened, Heaven and Earth seemed as one! As the notes of the song floated across the mountaintops, the villagers felt their hearts open to their highest dream, and each felt a long-lost hope return. When the villagers finished their prayers, they slowly opened their eyes. To their astonishment, where the old soldier had stood there was now a mighty tree. Perched in its boughs was a lovely white songbird singing her heartfelt song. Next to the mighty tree flowed a cool, clear stream. Everywhere the villagers looked they saw beautiful bushes, flowers, vines, and trees.

The garden was alive!

Gazing about the garden, the villagers slowly came to realize that each one of them had their own special place, and their own gift to give. And they saw that without each of them in their perfect place, the garden was incomplete. The heavenly scent of the lilies-of-the-valley filled the air. The bushes and vines were a haven for small mountain birds. The mighty tree offered comfort and shade, while the clear, cool stream nurtured the garden with its refreshing gift. The wildflowers, lilacs, and forget-me-nots filled the garden with blazing color, while the deep blue grasses and baby's breath swayed back and forth gently in the breeze.

As the sun rose over the mountains, the images of the garden began to fade, but no one in the village would ever be the same. Slowly opening her eyes, Mi Shan looked around and said, "What happened? I feel as though I have just awakened from the most beautiful dream!" At that moment, her gaze fell on her father, who was watching from a window in the inn. A radiant smile appeared on her face, and the words of her father echoed through the garden: "You must always keep your highest hope and highest dream alive within your heart. Remember, things are not always what they seem." Listening to those words, the villagers closed their eyes, for the vision of her father's garden was now alive within their hearts.

In the Great Cities, those who travel in the caravans still tell stories about the Village High Above the White Clouds. "It is a place," they say with a faraway look, "that is filled with peace. A place where everyone seems to have a special gift. A place," they grin sheepishly and say, "where all have a special hope and a special dream."

Some people in the Great Cities roll their eyes and shake their heads in disbelief. Yet others who hear the story feel something stir deep within, and set off up the mountain in search of their dream. Some turn back saying it is too hard a climb. But those who continue on toward the rugged mountain pass say they see a pure white songbird drifting in the high mountain winds, leading them on. And in the early morning light, just before night turns to day, they say they hear the notes of a song. "A song so beautiful," they whisper, "that it encourages us on."

"A song so wondrous," they
say with hope in their heart,
"that for a moment Heaven
and Earth seem as one."

Loving Kindness for Kids

Wisdom's children's books are available in bookstores or by calling

(800) 272-4050.

PRINCE SIDDHARTHA

The Story of Buddha
Jonathan Landaw
Illustrations by Janet Brooke

An inspiration for children of all ages.

This is the story of Prince Siddhartha and how he became Buddha, the Awakened One, told through lyrical prose. Beautiful full-color illustrations throughout depict each major life event in Siddhartha's development. Its message of harmlessness, loving-kindness, and unselfishness is vitally important for today's—and tomorrow's—children.
The story "…is presented with enough simplicity that a young reader has no trouble identifying with a child who lived so long ago and far away." —*Tricycle: The Buddhist Review*
144 pages, 8 x 10, full color throughout, $16.95, 0-86171-016-9

PRINCE SIDDHARTHA COLORING BOOK

A COMPANION BOOK TO PRINCE SIDDHARTHA
Drawings by Janet and Lara Brooke
Text by Jonathan Landaw

Thirty-one black-and-white line drawings give your child a chance to recreate in color the significant and formative events of the life of the young prince who became the Buddha. Now children can make this story of the development of universal love and compassion their own. A stand-alone companion volume to the illustrated book.
48 pages, 8H x 11, 31 full-size and 31 miniature line drawings, $6.95, 0-86171-121-1

THE GIFT

A Magical Story about Caring for the Earth
Written and illustrated by Isia Osuchowska

Long ago in a kingdom far away, Ananda, the Buddha's main student, taught a small-minded king the importance of sharing—not only one's personal wealth, but also the wealth of the earth's resources. Thirty vibrant watercolors illustrate this delightful children's tale about the importance of using nature's gifts wisely and altruistically.
32 pages, 8 x 8, full color throughout, case bound, $14.95, 0-86171-116-5